NBA CHAMPIONSHIPS:

NONE

ALL-TIME LEADING SCORER:

WALTER DAVIS (1977–88):

15,666 POINTS

THE NBA: A HISTORY OF HOOPS

PHOENIX SUNS

LAKERS
28

THE NBA: A HISTORY OF HOOPS

PHOENIX SUNS

BY JIM WHITING

CREATIVE EDUCATION CREATIVE PAPERBACKS

PHOENI
33

Published by Creative Education
and Creative Paperbacks

P.O. Box 227, Mankato, Minnesota 56002

Creative Education and Creative Paperbacks
are imprints of The Creative Company

www.thecreativecompany.us

Design by Blue Design; production by Joe Kahnke

Printed in the United States of America

Photographs by Alamy (REUTERS), AP Images (ASSOCIATED PRESS), Getty Images (Andrew D. Bernstein/NBAE, Vernon Biever/NBAE, Lisa Blumenfeld/Getty Images Sport, David Cannon, Jonathan Daniel/Stringer/Getty Images Sport, Hank Delespinasse/Sports Illustrated, Stephen Dunn/Allsport, Focus on Sport, Focus on Sport/Getty Images Sport, Rob Foldy/Getty Images Sport, Barry Gossage/NBAE, Andy Hayt/NBAE, Thearon W. Henderson/Getty Images Sport, Ronald Martinez/Getty Images Sport, John W. McDonough/Sports Illustrated, Fernando Medina/NBAE, Manny Millan/Sports Illustrated, NBAE, Christian Petersen/Getty Images Sport, Dick Raphael/Sports Illustrated, David Sherman/NBAE)

Library of Congress Cataloging-in-Publication Data

Names: Whiting, Jim, 1943- author.

Title: Phoenix Suns / Jim Whiting.

Series: The NBA: A History of Hoops.

Includes bibliographical references and index.

Summary: This high-interest title summarizes the history of the Phoenix Suns professional basketball team, highlighting memorable events and noteworthy players such as Steve Nash.

Identifiers: LCCN 2017006899 / ISBN 978-1-60818-858-1 (hardcover) / ISBN 978-1-62832-461-7 (pbk) / ISBN 978-1-56660-906-7 (eBook)

Subjects: LCSH: 1. Phoenix Suns (Basketball team)—History—Juvenile literature. 2. Phoenix Suns (Basketball team)—Biography—Juvenile literature.

Classification: LCC GV885.52.P47 W47 2017 / DDC 796.323/640979173—dc23

CCSS: RI.4.1, 2, 3, 4; RI.5.1, 2, 4; RI.6.1, 2, 3; RF.4.3, 4; RF.5.3, 4; RH. 6-8. 4, 5, 7

First Edition HC 9 8 7 6 5 4 3 2 1

First Edition PBK 9 8 7 6 5 4 3 2 1

PHX
DIAW
3
VANHORN
2

CONTENTS

Consistently hot and sunny, **PHOENIX** is often called "The Valley of the Sun."

GREATEST GAME . . . EVER?

Game 5 of the 1976 National Basketball Association (NBA) Finals looked dark for the Phoenix Suns. After just 9 minutes, they trailed the Boston Celtics 32–12. Many people were surprised

The Suns were hot in the 1976 Finals, but they could not outlast the Celtics.

the Suns were even here. They had barely qualified for the playoffs. The mighty Celtics had the best record in the Eastern Conference. A win tonight would give Boston a 3–2 series lead. Phoenix battled back. It tied the score as time expired. Each team scored six points in overtime. The game went to a second overtime. As it ended, the Celtics put up a shot that appeared to win the game, 111–110. Fans poured onto the floor. Not so fast, said the referees. One second remained. It took several minutes to clear the court. An enraged Boston fan attacked a referee. The Suns had to inbound the ball under their own basket. It would be nearly impossible to score.

Suns guard Paul Westphal had an idea. Call a timeout, he said. The Suns didn't have any remaining. It would be a technical foul. Boston would have a free throw. But the Suns would inbound at midcourt instead. They would have a better shot. Boston sank the free throw. Suns forward Gar Heard caught the inbounds pass. He spun around and launched a high, arching shot. It went in! Game tied—again. That meant a third overtime. Boston built an eight-point lead. Phoenix didn't give up. With 12 seconds left, it narrowed the score to 128–126. Westphal tried to steal the ball. He hoped to score and force a fourth overtime. He barely missed. Boston ran out the clock. "That was the most exciting basketball game I've ever seen," said broadcaster Rick Barry. "They just had one

BOSTON CELTICS 1964 WORLD CHAMPIONS
BOSTON CELTICS 1963 WORLD CHAMPIONS
BOSTON CELTICS 1962 WORLD CHAMPIONS
PHOENIX 18
CELTICS 17
CELTICS 18
SOBERS 40
PHOENIX 33
SUNS

great play after another.... It was such an emotional and physical game for everybody involved."

By the 1960s, the NBA was increasing in popularity. The league added Milwaukee and Phoenix in 1968. A Phoenix newspaper sponsored a name-the-team contest. Entries included Cactus Cowboys, Gila Monsters, Prickly Pears, Tarantulas, and White Wing Doves. Many, such as Sun Valley Pride and Sundials, reflected Arizona's year-round sunshine. Team officials went with Suns, the simplest version.

The team's first season in 1968–69 was mostly cloudy. Phoenix won just 16 games. But guards Gail Goodrich and Dick Van Arsdale both shone brightly. They each averaged more than 20 points a game. The poor record gave the Suns a chance at Lew Alcindor (later known as Kareem Abdul-Jabbar). Everyone knew he would be the top choice in the 1969 NBA Draft. But Phoenix lost a coin toss to Milwaukee. The

LEGENDS OF THE HARDWOOD

LEW-SING THE COIN FLIP

After their first year, the Suns and the Bucks ranked at the bottom of the standings. A coin toss would determine which picked first in the 1969 Draft. The winner would select superstar Lew Alcindor. A Phoenix newspaper held a poll to see what the Suns should call. "It was such a monumental, once-in-a-lifetime flip of a coin, why not let your fans be a part of that?" said general manager Jerry Colangelo. Heads, said the fans. The coin came up tails. Suns fans always wondered, "What if?" "We had a group of young guys that would have fit perfectly with Alcindor," said Colangelo. "We would have been in a prime position to have a good long run if we had won that coin flip."

LEGENDS OF THE HARDWOOD

OUT OF THE SHADOWS

CONNIE HAWKINS, FORWARD, 6-FOOT-8, 1969–74

As a college freshman, Connie Hawkins was accused of working with a gambler who paid players to lose games. Then the gambler bet on the other team. Both the university and the NBA banned Hawkins after that. So Hawkins played in the American Basketball League, the American Basketball Association, and with the Harlem Globetrotters. The NBA lifted his ban in 1969. Hawkins was an immediate sensation. He was a highflying leaper who averaged more than 24 points a game. "He was the first guy on that Dr. J, Michael Jordan level," said coach Doug Moe. "Long strides. Hold it in one hand. Wheel it around. Nobody could match him for that."

A member of the original Suns team, **DICK VAN ARSDALE** led Phoenix in scoring in 1970–71.

Bucks took Alcindor. The Suns added Connie Hawkins, a 27-year-old rookie. "Hawkins is a complete player," said New York Knicks coach Red Holzman. "You have to like him, because he plays both ends of the floor." Hawkins helped the Suns to 39 wins. Even though they still had a losing record, they qualified for the playoffs in 1970. They narrowly lost to the Los Angeles Lakers in the Western Division semifinals.

THE SUNS RISE

Phoenix did even better in the following two seasons. They won 48 and 49 games. But only the top two teams in each division made the playoffs. The Suns played in the league's Midwest Division then. Division rivals Milwaukee and Chicago finished ahead of them both seasons. Phoenix posted losing records the

More than 40 years later, **PAUL SILAS** still topped the Suns' career rebounders with 12.1 per game.

PAUL WESTPHAL led Phoenix to the Finals twice: in 1976 as a player and in 1993 as head coach.

next three seasons. The playoffs were becoming a distant memory.

Phoenix traded for Westphal before the 1975–76 season. It drafted center Alvan Adams. He was Rookie of the Year. Heard also became a Sun. It still took more than half the season for the team to gain traction. The Suns barely finished with a winning record, going 42–40. They caught fire in the playoffs. Phoenix beat the Seattle SuperSonics in the first round. Then it knocked off the defending NBA champion Golden State Warriors in seven games. After losing the first two games of the

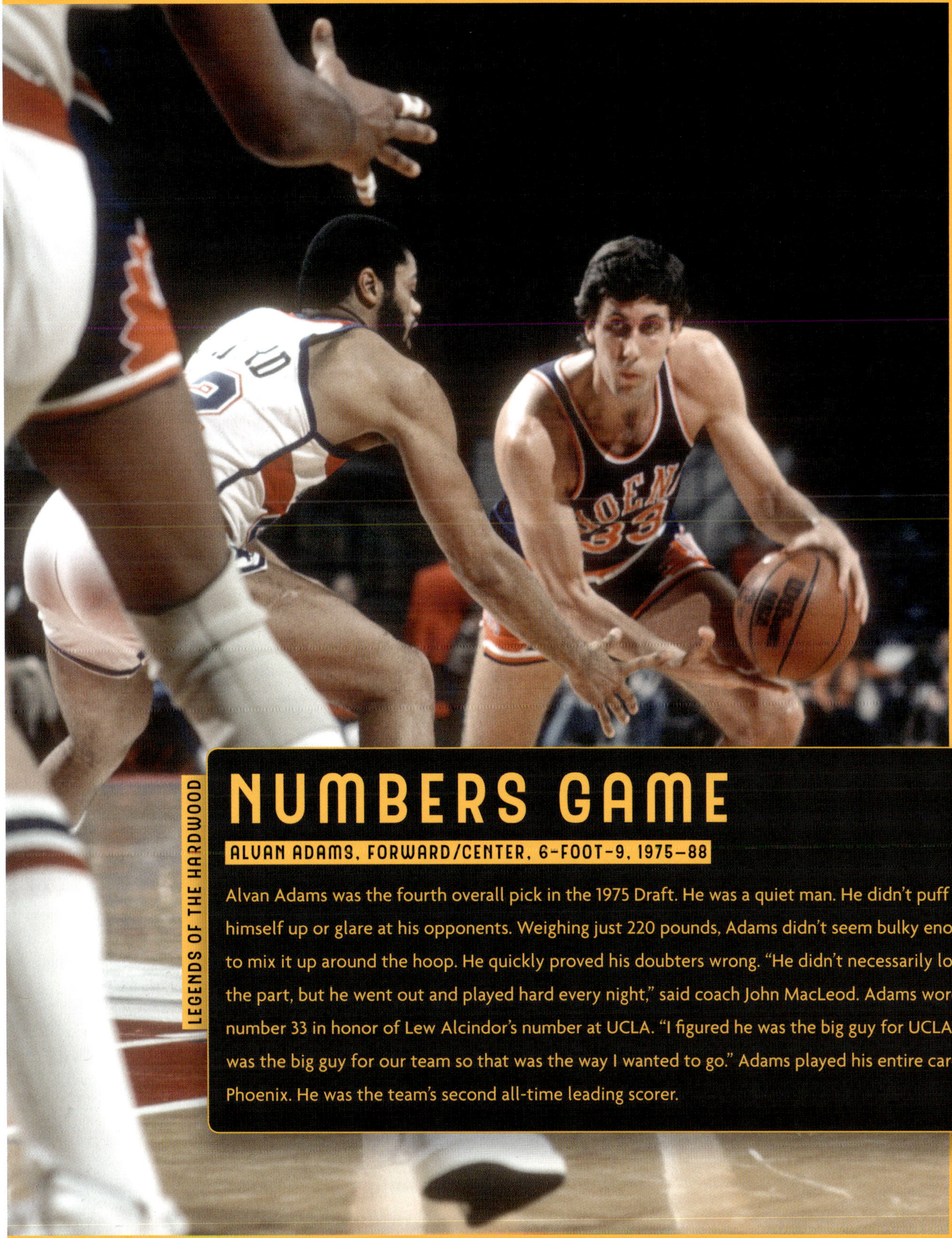

LEGENDS OF THE HARDWOOD

NUMBERS GAME

ALVAN ADAMS, FORWARD/CENTER, 6-FOOT-9, 1975–88

Alvan Adams was the fourth overall pick in the 1975 Draft. He was a quiet man. He didn't puff himself up or glare at his opponents. Weighing just 220 pounds, Adams didn't seem bulky enough to mix it up around the hoop. He quickly proved his doubters wrong. "He didn't necessarily look the part, but he went out and played hard every night," said coach John MacLeod. Adams wore number 33 in honor of Lew Alcindor's number at UCLA. "I figured he was the big guy for UCLA and I was the big guy for our team so that was the way I wanted to go." Adams played his entire career in Phoenix. He was the team's second all-time leading scorer.

Center and forward **ALVAN ADAMS** was a reliable presence on the court for 988 games over 13 years.

Finals to Boston, the Suns battled back to tie the series. That set the stage for the triple-overtime Game 5 and Heard's memorable shot. "It's a game that is always in our minds," Phoenix general manager Jerry Colangelo said years later. "It's one of the most historic games ever, and it's hard not to think about it." A Celtics surge late in Game 6 gave Boston the championship.

The Suns stumbled to 34 wins the following season. But they rebounded to 49 wins in 1977–78. Small forward Walter Davis was named Rookie of the Year. But the Suns lost in the first round of the playoffs. Phoenix had a franchise-best 50 wins the following season. It easily advanced to the Western Conference finals against the Sonics. After losing the first two games, Phoenix took the next three. It trailed by a point with less than a minute to go in Game 6 but missed three scoring opportunities. Seattle took a big lead in the decisive Game 7.

PHOENIX
33
CBS SPORTS

LEGENDS OF THE HARDWOOD

"GO"-ING APE

The Suns didn't have a mascot at first. A messenger from a singing telegram company came to a game in a gorilla suit in 1980. Team officials asked him to dance during timeouts. He was a hit. The team quickly made him the official mascot. Since then, "Go" raises the team flag to fire up fans. He makes spectacular dunks. He dances. He also appears at hundreds of local events every year. In 2005, Go became the first NBA mascot inducted into the Mascot Hall of Fame. Suns managing partner Robert Sarver said, "His induction ... merely confirms what we have always believed—The Gorilla is the best mascot of all time."

With graceful moves and a gentle touch, **WALTER "SWEET D" DAVIS** had a picture-perfect jump shot.

The Suns closed to within two points as the final seconds expired.

The Suns kept getting better. They had 55 wins in 1979–80. They won 57 games the following season. That was the best record in the Western Conference. They had early playoff exits both times. Their win total fell off a little in the next two seasons. Once again, they didn't last long in the playoffs. The Suns had a 41–41 record in 1983–84. This time, they caught fire in the playoffs. Phoenix won its first two series. It faced the heavily favored Lakers in the Western Conference finals. Los Angeles took a 3–1 series edge. Phoenix won Game 5. A last-second Phoenix shot fell just short in Game 6. The Lakers escaped with a 99–97 win to close out the series.

K. J. TO THE RESCUE

The Suns dipped to 36 wins the following season. Again they squeaked into the playoffs. Again they faced the Lakers. This time it was in the first round. Unlike the previous season, this series was no

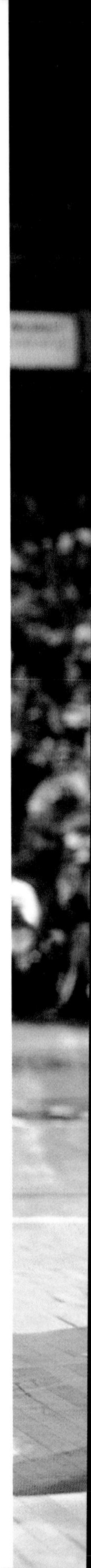

A leader on the floor, **KEVIN JOHNSON** could shoot, pass, and motivate his teammates.

contest. The Lakers averaged 136 points a game. They swept the series. Phoenix continued to decline in 1985–86. The Suns won just 32 games. They missed the playoffs for the first time in nine years. The playoffs remained out of the Suns' reach for two more seasons.

Suns officials overhauled the roster. The most important addition was point guard Kevin Johnson. "K. J.," as he quickly became known, arrived via a trade. He was a perfect fit. "It didn't take long to know that he was special," Colangelo said. "We knew he was a good player when we made the move, and he turned out to be better than we anticipated." He averaged more than 20 points and 12 assists a game in 1988–89. The league named him the Most Improved Player. Phoenix was also the most improved team. It went from 28 wins to 55. It was one of the biggest one-year turnarounds in NBA history.

JOHNSON averaged 15.9 points and 7 assists per game as the Suns eclipsed the Sonics to reach the 1993 Finals.

LEGENDS OF THE HARDWOOD

FINDING HIS NICHE

KEVIN JOHNSON, POINT GUARD, 6-FOOT-1, 1988–98, 1999–2000

As a boy, Kevin Johnson loved baseball. His high school friends talked him into playing basketball when he was a freshman. It was something to do in the winter when he wasn't playing baseball. It took two years to make the varsity team. "As a junior he was a baseball player who played basketball," said Ron McKenna, his basketball coach. "But by the time he was a senior, he came around and became a basketball player who played baseball." Baseball had one more shot. The Oakland A's drafted him before his senior year. But he stuck with basketball and set several school records. "He made the right decision," said A's scout Jim Guinn. Phoenix fans couldn't agree more.

Guard **GREG GRANT** spent his rookie season in Phoenix before moving on to other teams.

Unfortunately, Phoenix faced the Lakers again in the Western Conference finals. Los Angeles swept the series. But all four games were close. The largest margin of victory was just eight points. Phoenix finally turned the tables the following season. The Lakers had the best record in the NBA. The Suns beat them in the conference semifinals, four games to one. But they couldn't get by Portland in the next round. The Trail Blazers won the series 4–2. Johnson said, "We just needed to get a little stronger ... and find that toughness we needed."

Lanky forward **TOM CHAMBERS** topped the Suns in scoring for two years.

That toughness arrived three seasons later. The Suns traded for power forward Charles Barkley. Barkley was a ferocious rebounder and high scorer. The combination of K. J. and Barkley resulted in an NBA-best 62 wins. Barkley was named the league's Most Valuable Player (MVP). The Suns knocked off Seattle in the conference finals. Before the last game, Barkley promised 40 points and 20 rebounds. He lived up to his word. He

Fearless rebounder and shooter **CHARLES BARKLEY** inspired the Suns to rise.

A powerful Bulls squad put the squeeze on the Suns during the season and in the 1993 Finals.

had 44 points and pulled down 24 rebounds. "He'd carried this team so many times, and that game he came out and carried us," said teammate Dan Majerle. The Suns lost in the Finals to Michael Jordan and the Chicago Bulls, four games to two.

Phoenix continued playing well in the next two seasons. Both times it faced the Houston Rockets in the conference semifinals. Both times the Suns took a 3–2 lead. Both times the Rockets took the final two games. The Suns slid to 41 wins in 1995–96. They dropped to 40 the following season. By then Barkley was gone. Phoenix surged to 56 wins in 1997–98. But the San Antonio Spurs knocked the Suns out of the playoffs in the first round. Johnson retired.

THE CANADIAN SENSATION

Even without Johnson, the Suns continued playing at a high level for the next three years. One reason was forward Shawn Marion. He was the team's top draft pick in 1999. But Phoenix still

An athletic forward who could fill any role, **SHAWN MARION** flourished in Phoenix.

struggled to go deep in the playoffs. It missed the playoffs completely in 2001–02. It was the first time in 14 years the team finished the regular season without a playoff berth. Players such as power forward Amar'e Stoudamire helped the Suns return to the playoffs the following season. But they fell to just 29 wins in 2003–04.

The solution to the Suns' problems came soon after the end of the season. The team picked up Canadian-born All-Star point guard Steve Nash. He was not only a great shooter, but he also knew how to spread the ball around. Under his leadership on the court, the Phoenix offense became known as "seven seconds or less." That meant that the Suns were always on the go. They tried to shoot within seven seconds after gaining possession of the ball. Phoenix became one of the league's top-scoring teams. Its games were among the most exciting to watch.

"It was no secret as to how good Steve was before he got here," said coach Mike D'Antoni. "But once you see him operate day after day, it was a pretty awesome experience." That experience helped Phoenix surge to 62 wins in 2004–05. It was the best record in the league. Nash was named MVP. Phoenix made it all the way to the conference finals. But the team lost to the Spurs, four games to one. Nash repeated as MVP the following season. The Suns advanced to the conference finals again. This time they lost to the Dallas Mavericks, 4–2.

LEGENDS OF THE HARDWOOD

TIMING IS EVERYTHING

STEVE NASH, POINT GUARD, 6-FOOT-3, 1996–98, 2004–12

Steve Nash grew up in British Columbia, Canada. He began playing basketball in eighth grade and excelled in high school. He played at Santa Clara University. As a result, few Phoenix fans knew anything about him. Boos rained down when he was the Suns' top overall choice in 1996. "I probably would've booed myself too, but I'm going to be a really good player," he said then. Nash did little to justify that high choice for two years. He was traded to the Dallas Mavericks. He became a star. But the Mavericks had a lot of big contracts. They couldn't afford Nash. The Suns could. It was one of the best decisions in team history.

Superstar **SHAQUILLE O'NEAL** joined the Suns for two seasons but could not power them through the playoffs.

Nash nearly won a third straight MVP title in 2006–07. The Suns won 61 games that season. They bowed out in the conference semifinals. Hoping to get to the next level, the Suns added massive veteran center Shaquille O'Neal. He joined the team midway through the 2007–08 season. Phoenix went on to win 55 games that season. But it lost in the first round of the playoffs. The team's 46 wins the following season weren't good enough for the playoffs. O'Neal's bulk helped on defense. But he wasn't a good fit for the Suns' fast-break offense. He moved on.

Make your green game plan today.
aps.com
SIXERS
42
3
PHX
FULTON HOMES
BEST DEALS / BE
LESLIE'S
16
104

Knowledgeable and energetic, fan favorite **JARED DUDLEY** always made the right play.

SUNRISE, SUNSET

The Suns rose again in 2009–10. “I’d be happy to be part of a really positive, optimistic atmosphere, be a part of a team that is really on the same page, plays together, plays hard every night, and

Fifth pick in the 2013 Draft, 7-foot-1 center **ALEX LEN** nabbed 7.6 rebounds per game in 2015–16.

"I THOUGHT WE HAD A CHANCE TO DO SOMETHING SPECIAL. THIS IS AS SPECIAL A GROUP AS I'VE BEEN INVOLVED WITH.... I'D LOVE TO KEEP [THE TEAM] TOGETHER."

makes the season exciting for one another and for the fans," Nash said. He got his wish. Phoenix easily advanced to the Western Conference finals. But once again, the Lakers blocked further progress. Los Angeles took the series, four games to two. "I thought we had a chance to do something special," Nash said after the series. "This is as special a group as I've been involved with.... I'd love to keep [the team] together." This time he didn't get his wish. Several key players left. Phoenix missed the playoffs the next two seasons.

In 2012, the Suns traded Nash to the Lakers. In return, they got several high draft picks. Without his leadership, though, the team slumped to just 25 wins. Many experts thought Phoenix would do even worse in 2013–14. Yet it finished 48–34. One reason for the improvement was Eric Bledsoe. He joined the team at point guard and averaged nearly

18 points a game. The mark still wasn't quite good enough in the highly competitive Western Conference. Phoenix missed the playoffs by just one game. It didn't come close the following season. The Suns won only 39 games. Things got even worse in 2015–16. Bledsoe was injured early in the season. Though they added Brandon Knight at point guard, the Suns played below expectations. They won only 23 games. It also marked the sixth straight year in which Phoenix failed to reach the playoffs. That was the longest playoff drought in team history.

The drought continued in 2016–17. With just 24 wins, Phoenix had the worst record in the Western Conference and second-worst overall. But second-year shooting guard Devin Booker scored 70 points in a game against Boston. He was just the sixth player to reach that mark. Athletic power forward Marquese Chriss had a strong rookie season.

The city of Phoenix was originally named Pumpkinville. Fittingly, it didn't take the Suns long to become Cinderella. They turned their pumpkin into an elegant carriage that carried them to the playoffs. In recent years, though, the clock seemed to strike midnight. The Suns were back to scrubbing pots while their sister teams were dancing in the postseason. Phoenix fans hoped their team would soon find another glass slipper and rejoin the playoff ball.

Young shooting guard **DEVIN BOOKER** showed his ability to put up points in 2016–17.

SELECTED BIBLIOGRAPHY

Ballard, Chris. *The Art of a Beautiful Game: The Thinking Fan's Tour of the NBA*. New York: Simon & Schuster, 2010.

Hareas, John. *Ultimate Basketball: More Than 100 Years of the Sport's Evolution*. New York: DK, 2004.

Hubbard, Jan, ed. *The Official NBA Basketball Encyclopedia*. 3rd edition. New York: Doubleday, 2000.

NBA.com. "Phoenix Suns." http://www.nba.com/suns/.

Simmons, Bill. *The Book of Basketball: The NBA According to the Sports Guy*. New York: Ballantine, 2009.

Sports Illustrated. *Sports Illustrated Basketball's Greatest*. New York: Sports Illustrated, 2014.

WEBSITES

JR. NBA
http://jr.nba.com/

This kids site has games, videos, game results, team and player information, statistics, and more.

NBA'S 60 GREATEST PLAYOFF MOMENTS #6: '76 FINALS (CELTICS - SUNS)
https://www.youtube.com/watch?v=AcXtjt2bMUw

This video shows Gar Heard's famous shot in the 1976 NBA Finals. The clip is followed by a longer one showing the confusion surrounding the final moments of the second overtime and ending with Heard's shot.

Note: Every effort has been made to ensure that any websites listed above were active at the time of publication. However, because of the nature of the Internet, it is impossible to guarantee that these sites will remain active indefinitely or that their contents will not be altered.

INDEX